Princess Evangeline

Written by: S. N. Wilson

Illustrated by: Natalie Marino

xulon
PRESS

Dedicated to my beloved Evangeline. May you always see
the world as it could be and not just as it is.
May you continue to spread joy and imagination
everywhere you go.

In a kingdom all of her own making, lives a princess named Evangeline. This young princess is sweet and clever. She loves her family and her friends. She adores the color purple. Princess Evangeline sees the world for all of its wonderful possibilities. She wakes up every morning with a cheerful smile on her face.

Princess Evangeline enjoys mornings. She greets the rising
sun with much enthusiasm. Each morning Evangeline puts on
her royal purple robes. She peers into the mirror to make sure
that her tiara and dress fits just right. Then she hurries to
wake the people of her kingdom.

Evangeline travels through her kingdom in her royal chariot
with her loyal court jester, Mungo. The considerate young lady
makes sure that her subjects always awake bright and early to
much merry making.

Evangeline enjoys making art to share with the people of her kingdom. Once the princess drew a portrait of her family on the wall of the banquet hall.

She smiled happily at the looks of joy on the faces of her parents and grandmother as they gazed at her beautiful wall mural. Even Mungo looked impressed at the image of himself.

Sarah is Princess Evangeline's best friend and royal advisor. She and her mother, Duchess Jessica, come for their royal play-date. As the royal advisor, it is Sarah's job to recommend activities to brighten up the kingdom. Sarah always has great suggestions. Whenever an idea strikes, Sarah's green eyes light up with impish glee.

One day Sarah came up with a great idea.

While playing in the royal courtyards, the girls saw wild
flowers blooming near the walls surrounding the kingdom.
Sarah clapped her hands together and jumped up and down
joyfully. Sarah was sure that the Queen Mother and the
Duchess would love a bouquet of roses as a gift of love. So she
and Princess Eva clipped some of the blooms and put them
into baskets.

When the girls gave the flowers to the women, the Queen Mother and Duchess Jessica were so amazed they could not speak.

The Queen Mother and the Duchess ran excitedly
to the edge of the kingdom.
The Queen Mother was so moved that her eyes
welled up with tears.
Evangeline never forgot the look of wonder on her mother's
face as she gazed at the flower bushes.

Reigning over an empire can keep a princess very busy. There is much kingdom business to accomplish every day.

Mungo needs daily exercise.

There are chores to complete.

Evangeline's subjects come to her as she sits on her royal throne.
Her people often have many requests.
Princess Evangeline does her best to do as her people ask of her.

The Queen Mother likes to have visitors at the palace. So it is very important to her to make sure that the palace is a very comfortable place to visit. It pleases her very much when Evangeline helps to keep the palace neat and tidy.

Even Mungo requests that the Princess plays his favorite games. Playtime helps to lift his spirit so that he can perform tricks to amuse the royal family and their guests.

There are also appointments to keep. Some of them are fun.

And some appointments are not so fun.

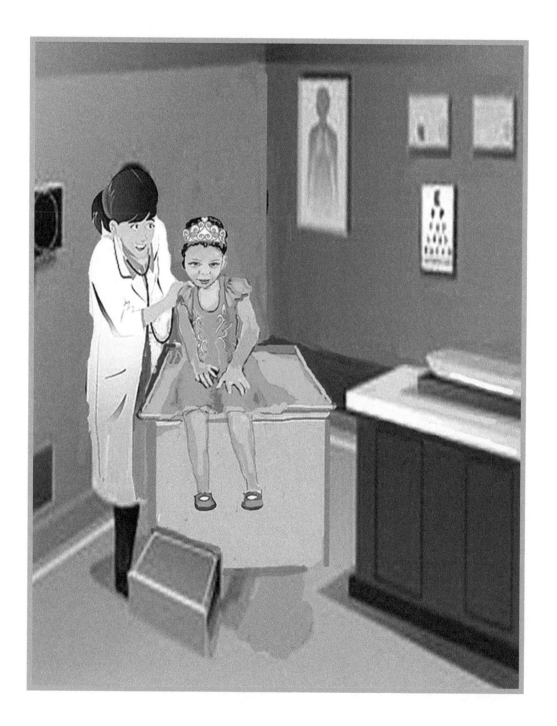

Of course, even with a full calendar, Princess Evangeline is sure to spend time with family.
The Queen Mother and the Grand Mother prepare a delicious feast. Then they all sit down at the banquet table and talk about their day.

After the feast, it is time for the evening entertainment.
Mungo humors the princess and Queen Mother with antics he
learned at court jesters' academy.

As the sun begins to set, the princess yawns and stretches.
Bedtime is fast approaching.

To help the princess calm down after a long day,
she relaxes in a huge, warm spa of bubbles.

Fed, bathed, and tucked snugly into bed, Evangeline is ready for story time. This is her favorite part of the day. The Queen Mother delights Evangeline with tales of other princesses and their adventures.

The princess listens intently. Soon her eyes become so heavy
she cannot keep them open.
The Queen Mother's voice floats gently through Eva's mind as
the princess drifts off to dreamland.

Mungo gets ready for bed, too. He lies down in his bed in the royal chambers. As Princess Evangeline turns in for the night, Mungo thinks of his fun days at the royal court jesters' academy.

The Queen Mother kisses the sleeping princess goodnight. Then she turns out the light and tiptoes quietly out of the room, leaving the princess and the court jester to spend the night dreaming away.

After all, tomorrow is a brand new day and full of the possibility of all new adventures.

Things to consider for discussion...

1. Evangeline loves mornings and wakes up with a cheerful smile on her face. Do you love mornings? What is your favorite time of the day?
2. Evangeline draws on the wall. Do you think that her family was really happy about that? What makes you think that?
3. If you had to choose a friend to be your royal advisor, who would that person be? Does this person think of fun things for you to do together- or are you the one who does that?
4. Evangeline uses her imagination to make ordinary activities fun. Which of these activities do you do also? How do you use your imagination during your day?
5. Evangeline imagines that she is a princess. If you could be anyone, who would you imagine yourself to be?